THIS BOOK BELONGS

TO _Tenisha Diane Brown_

DISNEY'S
SMALL WORLD LIBRARY
GOOFY TAKES OFF
An Adventure in Switzerland

GROLIER ENTERPRISES INC.

DANBURY, CONNECTICUT

© The Walt Disney Company. All rights reserved.
Printed in the United States of America.
Developed by The Walt Disney Company in conjunction with Nancy Hall, Inc.
ISBN: 0-7172-8222-8

Morty and Ferdie hopped out of the horse-drawn sleigh just as it pulled up outside their hotel in Switzerland. They had been looking forward to their winter holiday in the snow-covered Alps for quite some time.

"Uncle Mickey, may we go play with those kids over there?" asked Morty, pointing to some children who were building a snowman.

"Sure," said Mickey. He turned to Goofy as the boys happily ran off. "They're certainly not wasting any time. Let's hurry up and check into the hotel—maybe we'll have time for some fun in the snow before dinner!"

"Sounds good, Mick!" Goofy replied.

Fritz and Margrit Strauss introduced themselves to Morty and Ferdie.

"And this is our baby brother, Hans," Margrit said as a smaller boy ran to join them.

"I'm not a baby!" Hans said huffily.

"Right," said Fritz, smiling. "In fact, you're such a big boy, you can help us build the snowman!"

Hans happily agreed, and soon the children were hard at work.

Just as they were putting the finishing touches on the snowman, Mickey and Goofy came out of the hotel.

"There's been a mistake," said Mickey worriedly. "Our room isn't available until tomorrow night."

"But where will we stay tonight?" asked Ferdie.

"You can stay with us," said a smiling man with twinkling eyes.

"Papa!" said Margrit. She turned to Morty and Ferdie. "Oh, do come home with us! We'll have so much fun!"

"Thank you very much," said Mickey to Mr. Strauss. "If you're sure it isn't any trouble, we'd love to stay with you tonight."

Mr. Strauss led the group back to his house. Mrs. Strauss was happy to meet their guests. She quickly added four more plates to the table.

"What a great way to eat!" said Ferdie, as he dipped his bread into a pot of melted cheese.

After dinner, everyone drank hot chocolate by the fire.

"There's a ski-jump competition tomorrow," said Mr. Strauss. "Would you like to watch it with us?"

"We'd love to," said Mickey.

"Then you'll see me," said Hans. "I'm going to jump the farthest," he added proudly.

The whole family chuckled. "Oh, Hans," said Margrit. "You know you're much too little to go ski jumping."

But Hans had already made up his mind.

The next morning everyone went to the ski area.
While Mr. and Mrs. Strauss went skiing with Hans, Fritz
and Margrit tried to teach Morty and Ferdie how to ski.

"Gawrsh, Mickey," said Goofy, pointing at Hans skiing
by. "Look how well Hans can ski! It doesn't look too hard.
I think I'll give it a try."

"It takes a lot of practice, Goofy," warned Mickey. "I've been skiing for a long time, and I'm still not as good as Hans."

"I bet I can do it," said Goofy. "Watch this!" He tried to ski down the slope, but he didn't get very far. Both his legs shot straight up in the air.

"On second thought," said Goofy, "maybe I will join Morty and Ferdie's lesson."

"I think that's a good idea," said Mickey. "I'll go catch up with Mr. and Mrs. Strauss."

Fritz and Margrit were good teachers. In no time at all, Morty, Ferdie, and Goofy had learned how to "snowplow," which is what beginning skiers do when they want to turn or stop.

"Look at me!" called Goofy proudly as he skied down the beginners' slope. "Now I'm ready to ski down from the top of the mountain."

"I don't think so, Goofy," said Fritz. "The top of the mountain is only for expert skiers."

"Don't worry," said Goofy confidently. "I'll take it nice and slow."

Soon Goofy was sailing through the sky in the ski lift. He looked down and saw Mickey with Mr. and Mrs. Strauss and Hans.

"See you later at the ski-jump competition!" Goofy called.

"I hope he knows what he's doing," said Mickey to the others in a worried voice.

Hans waved to Goofy. "You'll see me at the competition," he thought to himself. "I'm going to be the winner!"

Goofy finally arrived at the top of the mountain. He skied over to the start of the slope and looked down.

"Gawrsh!" he said. "It sure looks steep! Maybe I don't belong here, after all."

But before Goofy could change his mind, he lost his balance. Suddenly he found himself heading straight down the slope!

"Whoa!" he shouted. "Where are the brakes?" He was going so fast that he couldn't control his skis.

"Watch out!" he yelled, as the other skiers scrambled to get out of his way.

Somehow Goofy managed to stay upright as he plunged down the mountain. Little by little the trail became less steep. As Goofy slowed down, he found himself heading toward a little village.

"I must have skied right out of the ski area," he thought. "I'll have to ask someone how to get back."

Goofy came to a stop in front of a chocolate shop. A woman standing in the doorway saw Goofy's puzzled expression and asked him if he needed any help.

"I'm supposed to be at the ski-jump competition," said Goofy sheepishly. "Do you know how to get there?"

"Oh, yes," said the woman. "As a matter of fact, we're giving a box of chocolates to the winner of the contest. Would you like to try one of our chocolates?" she asked.

Goofy took off his skis and followed the woman into the shop. Then he took one of the chocolates.

"Gawrsh!" he said. "This is the best chocolate I've ever tasted."

"Yes, Switzerland is known for its fine chocolates," the woman told him. Then she gave Goofy directions to the competition.

Goofy tried to follow the directions, but in no time at all he was lost again, this time finding himself in front of a store that sold clocks and watches.

Goofy took off his skis and stepped in the front door. "Can you tell me how to get to the ski-jump competition?" he asked one of the workers.

"Certainly!" said the man. "In fact, the winner of today's competition will be presented with one of our beautiful watches," he added proudly, showing Goofy a pocket watch. Goofy looked at the time.

"Oh, no!" he exclaimed. "I'm going to miss the competition!"

"If you hurry, you can still make it," the worker assured him. He gave Goofy directions for a short cut.

Goofy skied to the edge of the village and looked down a steep hill.

"There's the competition!" he said. "I think I can even see Mickey."

As Goofy leaned over a little more for a better look, he felt himself losing his balance. Before he knew it, he was sailing down the hill.

"Here I go again!" Goofy shouted.

At the competition, Mr. and Mrs. Strauss and Mickey met up with Fritz, Margrit, Morty, and Ferdie.

"Where is Hans?" a concerned Mrs. Strauss asked the children. "He told us he was going to ski with you for a while."

Fritz and Margrit looked at each other. "We haven't seen him since this morning," said Fritz.

Mickey was also worried. "Goofy should be here by now, too," he said to the others.

But while Goofy was plunging down the hill, Hans was headed up to the top of the ski jump. "Once everyone sees what a good jumper I am, they'll never call me a baby again," he said to himself.

Hans sneaked in behind one of the ski jumpers. He was just about to take off down the jump when he heard a familiar voice calling "HELP!"

"What's he doing?" Hans thought as he caught sight of Goofy skiing out of control. "Someone needs to save him!"

Hans didn't hesitate. He left the ski jump and quickly headed down the trail.

In no time at all, Hans was skiing alongside Goofy.

"Boy, am I glad to see you!" Goofy shouted.

Hans did a snowplow turn. "Turn your skis like mine," he called to Goofy.

Goofy did as Hans told him, and he began to slow down. Everybody in the ski area watched in amazement as Goofy and Hans arrived safely at the bottom of the hill.

The Strauss family and Mickey ran over to them.

"Are you all right?" Mr. Strauss asked Hans and Goofy.

Goofy just grinned. "We're fine!" he said. "Why, little Hans here saved me in the nick of time!"

Hans frowned at Goofy. "You shouldn't have been on that trail," Hans told him. "You could have hurt yourself."

"Gawrsh, Hans," said Goofy. "I'm sorry. I guess I just wanted to prove to everyone that I was a great skier, but skiing is sure a lot harder than it looks!"

"Hans," said Mr. Strauss, "what were you doing at the top of the mountain?"

Hans looked down sheepishly. "I guess I made a mistake, too," he said. "But I just wanted to show everyone that I'm not a baby."

"Hans," said Mrs. Strauss, "you're not a baby, but you're still a little boy. And Goofy is just learning to ski. In time, you will get bigger, and Goofy will become a better skier. You both have to be patient."

Just then the judge of the competition rushed over to shake Hans's hand. "You're a real hero!" he said.

"Not bad for a little boy!" Fritz said, winking at his brother. Then everyone laughed as they walked back to watch the ski-jump competition.

Did You Know...?

There are many different customs and places that make each country special. Do you remember some of the things below from the story?

The Swiss Alps are part of Europe's highest mountain chain. Swiss people enjoy skiing and bobsledding on these beautiful snow-capped peaks in winter and climbing and camping on them in summer.

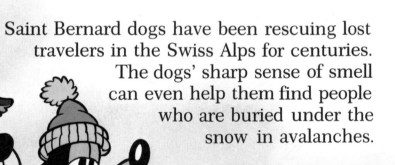

Saint Bernard dogs have been rescuing lost travelers in the Swiss Alps for centuries. The dogs' sharp sense of smell can even help them find people who are buried under the snow in avalanches.

Fondue is a favorite Swiss dish made of melted cheese in which pieces of bread or vegetables are dipped. The bowl sits over a flame that keeps it hot. People pop the cheese-covered bread into their mouths. What a delicious treat!

Swiss chocolates are among the best in the world. The Swiss make hundreds of different types of chocolate, and almost every Swiss town has at least one chocolate shop.

Yodeling is a popular kind of Swiss folk singing. Yodeling probably grew out of Swiss farmers' cattle calls hundreds of years ago. The yodeling sound is meant to imitate a voice echoing off mountain walls.

A favorite Swiss game is Hornussen (HOR-nus-sin). This game is similar to baseball but there are some big differences. Instead of a bat and a ball, the batter uses an eight-foot-long club to hit a wooden disk. The disk is caught by players with wooden rackets.

Skiing is a popular sport in Switzerland.
Many Swiss children learn to ski about the
same time they learn to walk!

German, French, and Italian are the official languages
of Switzerland. Each is spoken in a different region of
the country. *Romansh* (roh-MANCH), the fourth
national language, is actually spoken by only a
few Swiss people. "Guten Tay" (GOU-ten TAY),
"Allo" (AH-low), and "Ciao" (CHOW) all mean hello
in Switzerland.

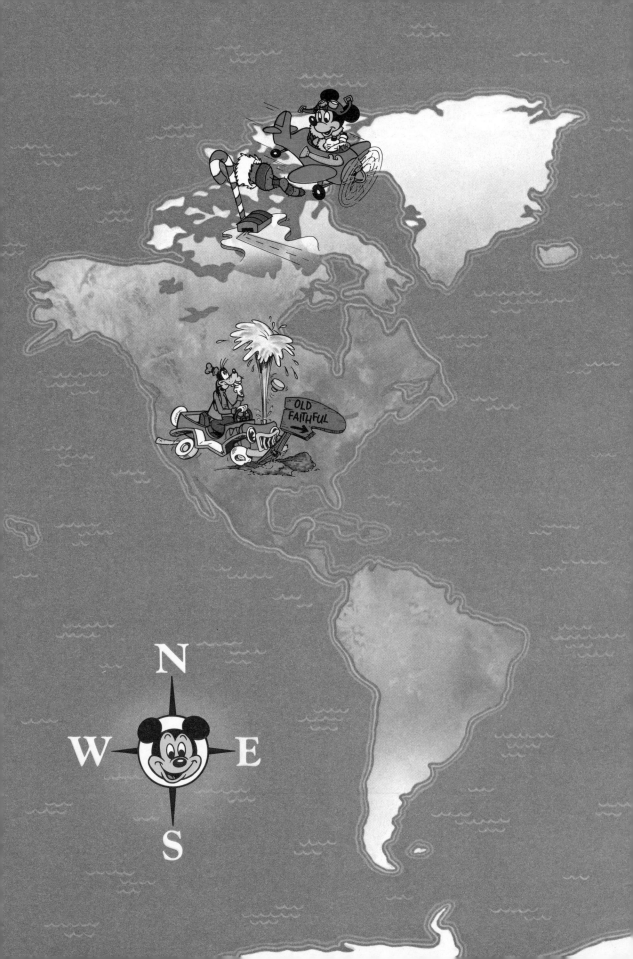